Around the Year

Around the Year

Tasha Tudor

Simon & Schuster Books for Young Readers

New York   London   Toronto   Sydney   Singapore

SIMON & SCHUSTER BOOKS FOR YOUNG READERS

An imprint of Simon & Schuster Children's Publishing Division

1230 Avenue of the Americas

New York, New York, 10020

Text copyright 1957 by Oxford University Press

Copyright renewed ©1985 by Corgi Cottage, L.L.C.

First Simon & Schuster Books for Young Readers edition, 2001

All rights reserved including the right of reproduction in whole or in part in any form.

SIMON & SCHUSTER BOOKS FOR YOUNG READERS is a trademark of Simon & Schuster.

Book design by Anahid Hamparian

The illustrations are rendered in watercolor and ink.

Printed in Hong Kong

2 4 6 8 10 9 7 5 3 1

Library of Congress Control Number:2001087011

ISBN 0-689-82847-0

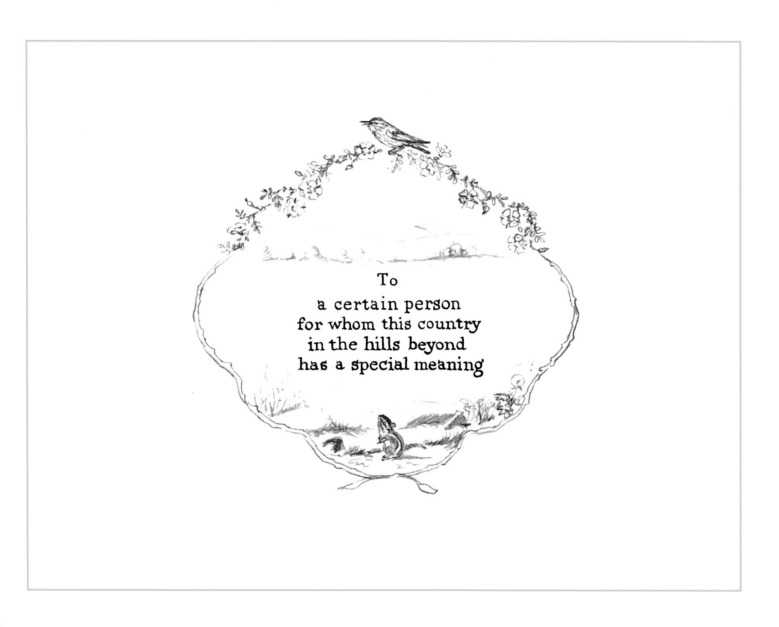

To
a certain person
for whom this country
in the hills beyond
has a special meaning

January brings us

coasting,

Taffy pulls and apple roasting.

Chill **February**

brings the day,

When hearts and flowers

we give away.

March promises

the hope of spring,

In swampy places peepers sing.

April sees the birds return,

Scatters showers

on leaf and fern.

May brings us

armfuls of delight,

Bird-song, warm sun

and gardens bright.

In June comes

summer's longest day,

Now meadows smell

of new-mown hay.

Hot **July** brings picnic joys,

Firecrackers for girls and boys.

In August

swallows southward fly,

Summer's waning, fall is nigh.

September brings the Country Fair,

Falling leaves,

crisp autumn air.

October brings us

Halloween,

When witches, ghosts

and spooks are seen.

November brings

good skating weather,

Thanksgiving gathers us together.

December brings

glad Christmas cheer,

May joy be yours

AROUND THE YEAR.

January brings us coasting,
Taffy pulls and apple roasting.

Chill February brings the day,
When hearts and flowers we give away.

March promises the hope of spring,
In swampy places peepers sing.

April sees the birds return,
Scatters showers on leaf and fern.

May brings us armfuls of delight,
Bird-song, warm sun and gardens bright.

In June comes summer's longest day,
Now meadows smell of new-mown hay.

Hot July brings picnic joys,
Firecrackers for girls and boys.

In August swallows southward fly,
Summer's waning, fall is nigh.

September brings the Country Fair,
Falling leaves, crisp Autumn air.

October brings us Halloween,
When witches, ghosts and spooks are seen.

November brings good skating weather,
Thanksgiving gathers us together.

December brings glad Christmas cheer,
May joy be yours AROUND THE YEAR.

Two-time Caldecott honor artist *Tasha Tudor* is one of America's most renowned illustrators of children's books. Her watercolor depictions of Americana are famous throughout the world. And ***Around the Year*** evokes a seasonal wonderland in signature Tudor style. Here flowers, firecrackers, and fall leaves spirit readers on a journey back to a quieter, simpler time. Tudor's native New England and her own family history inspired many of these cherished holiday traditions. While today's landscapes are seldom as idyllic as Tudor's world, the fundamentals of our happiness—caring, family, friendship, anticipation, and celebration—remain the same. These elements endow Tudor's art with its timeless warmth, ensuring her work will be enjoyed for generations to come.